To Emily, George and John
C.B.

British Library Cataloguing in Publication Data

Butterworth, Christine, *1945-*
The sand dolphin.
I. Title   II Broadley, Susan
823.914[J]

ISBN 0-340-52853-2

First published 1990

Published by Hodder and Stoughton Children's Books,
a division of Hodder and Stoughton Ltd,
Mill Road, Dunton Green, Sevenoaks, Kent TN13 2YA

Printed in Hong Kong

The Sand Dolphin

Christine Butterworth

Illustrations by Sue Broadley

HODDER AND STOUGHTON
LONDON SYDNEY AUCKLAND TORONTO

All over the beach children were busy building sandcastles. Mary wanted to make something different, so she found a quiet part of the beach where the sand was cool, damp and smooth. There were no footprints in the sand because this part of the beach was washed by the sea when the tide came in.

Mary scooped up handfuls of soft, grainy sand and made a long mound. She piled on more sand and smoothed it into a rounded hump. The afternoon passed as she worked. Shadows on the beach grew longer. Some of the children went home.

The hump grew and lengthened into a curved body. A head with a long blunt nose grew out of one end. The other end tapered into a graceful tail. Two limpet shells pushed in for eyes, and it was done. Mary smoothed her sand dolphin from head to tail and gave its sides a pat.

She wrote her name on it with her finger,
M A R Y.

'My sand dolphin,' she said. Then she heard
her mother call, and the two of them went
home up the cliff path. As the beach emptied, the
tide began to come in.

That night Mary went to sleep with her window open to hear the sound of the sea. As the evening star came out, the waves lapped across the smooth sand. The tide was coming up the beach.

When the night was dark, the moon made a silver path over the sea water to where small waves licked at the tail of the sand dolphin. The foam at the edge of a wave washed over the limpet shell eyes. They began to gleam in the dark.

As the water rose higher still the sand dolphin slipped into the sea. Mary turned over but did not wake up.

When the night was at its darkest, the waves reached high up the beach. Even the largest rocks were under water. The sand dolphin slid in and out of the strands of seaweed that grew on the rocks. It swam deep inside secret flooded caves where only crabs and lobsters lived.

For a time the sand dolphin played hide and seek with tiny silver fish, their scales gleaming in the moonlight. It swam up to the surface to race the tall green breakers as they swept towards the shore.

Then the first streaks of light showed in the sky. The sand dolphin felt a pull as the tide turned. With a flick of its strong tail, it swam steadily out to where the deep bed of the sea lay always in shadow.

In her warm bed at the top of the cliffs, Mary swam up from her deep sleep to the noisy surface of daytime. She hurried down to the beach before breakfast, her feet making the first marks of the day on the smooth sand. There was just one thing she wanted to find. She came to the place where she had made her sand dolphin but it was not there.

'The best thing I ever made,' she said, 'and it's all gone.'

Later in the day, she took her mother to see the place.

'Of course it's not there any more,' said her mother. 'What did you expect? The tide comes right over here.'

'But even the limpet shell eyes have gone,' said Mary.

'Never mind, you can make another dolphin,' said her mother. Mary sighed. Her mother did not understand.

For the rest of the morning Mary sat by her
mother, silent and sad, playing fivestones with a
handful of pebbles. Later she played noisy games
with her friends.

'Good,' thought her mother. 'Mary's not upset
any more.'

But after Mary had said goodbye to her friends
at the end of the day and was getting ready for
bed, she still felt a sad empty corner inside.

That second night, as the tide came up higher still to cover the tall dark rocks, the sand dolphin returned. It swam once more through scarves of waving seaweed as crabs scuttled over the sandy floor. Purple anemones moved a million tiny tentacles as the waves broke far above them on the surface of the sea, as smooth as a green glass table. This time Mary saw the sand dolphin in her dreams.

Her fingers stirred gently in her sleep like the anemone's tentacles. She smiled, her eyes tight shut as she saw how beautifully her sand dolphin could swim. She watched the moonlight catch its milky grey sides as it rolled over and over on the surface of the sea.

When she awoke, she lay for a long time with her eyes shut to keep hold of the dream for a little longer – but her sand dolphin had swum out of sight. Even so, the happy feeling that had come with the dream stayed with her as she got out of bed. She was not sad now because she knew her sand dolphin had gone home to the sea.

The third day on the beach, Mary began to build something bigger than ever before. She dug a long deep hole that came to a point at one end. Then she made stout sides that rose up around a hollow inside. At lunch-time her mother came to look.

'What a splendid boat!' she said admiringly. Mary nodded, too busy to talk.

She built a sturdy seat of firm sand in the middle of the boat, and decorated the sides with swirling patterns of shells and coloured pebbles. The final touch was a long string of glossy brown seaweed trailing from the bows.

All the way up the cliff path going home, Mary could see her boat. As they climbed higher it shrank until it was the size of a toy.

All evening Mary was impatient for night to come. As the dark clouds rolled inland, she went to bed. The sighing and sucking noises made by the waves far below came in at her window as she closed her eyes. She fell asleep at once, with her fingers curled round her most precious shell. The evening star lit the dark blue sky and was followed by the moon as the night grew blacker. Moonlight threw a silver path across the sea and came through a gap in Mary's curtains to touch her face.

Mary found herself on the beach. The waves were already lapping at her sand boat. She stepped in and sat down. The sea around the sides of the boat grew deeper. Without knowing the moment when it happened, Mary felt the boat begin to bob up and down as the waves rolled in under it.

She peered into the dark out to sea. Was that a faint sound? Without warning, there was a sharp tug as the string of seaweed tied at the bows stretched tight. Mary knew at once who had come to pull the boat. The sand dolphin's broad grey head bobbed in front of the bows. It had the seaweed rope in its mouth and was towing the boat swiftly through the water.

They gathered speed, creaming a wave along their sides, boat and dolphin, as they rushed along. The cool, salty night wind brushed Mary's cheeks, and she laughed aloud as they sped over the water.

The dolphin followed the silver path of moonlight for a while, and then slowed down. Its grey head turned to look at Mary as it let go of the rope of seaweed and dived under the waves. Mary did not hesitate. She stood up in the boat, took a deep breath and dived too, following the dolphin into the warm dark sea.

As she came back to the surface, she felt something nudge her shoulder. The dolphin leaned towards her and she climbed on to its back. Again the two of them followed the path of moonlight across the water. The dolphin arched its strong back and leapt into the air, carrying Mary, then dived cleanly through the water with hardly a splash.

They played until the moonlight began to
fade. Then the dolphin carried Mary back to
shallow water, where the sand sloped up into
the beach below the cliffs, and gently put her
down. Mary put her arms round the dolphin and
whispered 'Thank you' before paddling into
shore. She turned to wave, but the dolphin was
already out of sight. Mary peered far out to sea,
but all she could see were the first streaks of light
which meant day was starting.

'Come on sleepyhead, time to get up.' Her mother pulled back the curtains and warm sunlight fell on Mary's face. She sat up in bed blinking, trying to remember where she was. Outside her window, the sea was a bright morning green. Her hand still clasped the shell she had held all night. She put it to her ear to hear the sighing of the sea – and from far away heard the faint splash of a dolphin diving away from the light into the deep, grey-green shadows.